OLD MACDONALD HEARD A PARP FROM THE PAST

For Tuesday and Cissy

First published in paperback in Great Britain by HarperCollins *Children's Books* in 2018

1 3 5 7 9 10 8 6 4 2

ISBN: 978-0-00-824156-8

HarperCollins *Children's Books* is a division of HarperCollins*Publishers* Ltd.

Visit our website at www.harpercollins.co.uk

Printed and bound in China

OLD MACDONALD HEARD A PARP FROM THE PAST

Olaf Falafel

HarperCollins *Children's Books*

Old MacDonald had a farm...
E-I-E-I-O!

But life was boring on the farm -
He longed for a new place to go.

The bearded farmer had a great plan
And with some help from his team,
They used fancy parts
And a tank full of parps
To make a time-travelling machine.

His tractor was
joined to the tower

And lightning
struck with a blast...

And as the bell chimed

They travelled through time

To find the best parps from the past.

Our hero looked at the big shiny dial –
He pulled the lever and span it!

With a moo and a quack
They'd travelled way back...

To when dinosaurs
lived on our planet.

Old MacDonald heard a parp...
E-I-E-I-O!

With a Brrrp Brrrp here

and a Brrrp Brrrp there...

Keep your lips together and blow out as hard as you can.

Make your mouth erupt like a volcano.

It was now time to go!

Ancient Egypt was
where they stopped next.

They soon found a
good place to park.

And a beautiful queen
With jewels red and green

Let out the most
ladylike parp.

Old MacDonald heard a parp...
E-I-E-I-O!

Make your mouth as small as you can, and suck on an imaginary straw.

and a Wwbb Wwbb there...

It was now time to go!

The tractor came
to a screeching halt

By a camp in a
muddy old field,

And the Viking chief
To much disbelief
Squeezed a parp out
from under his shield.

Old MacDonald heard a parp...
E-I-E-I-O!

With a Pwwrb

Pwwrb here...

Pwwrb!

Squeeze air out of
one side of your mouth,

and make a noise like
a frog with a kazoo.

It was now time to go!

The adventurous farmer kept moving on
Through some hilarious scenes,

Like a flatulent Inca,

A right royal stinker...

And a cowgirl who'd filled up on beans.

Our fearless gang had made it in time
To witness man land on the moon,

But he parped and he cursed
Because they were there first
And his suit filled up like a balloon.

Old MacDonald had a farm...
E-I-E-I-O!

And with their tractor low on fuel,
Now was the time to head home.

But as they journeyed
back through the years

They heard the
most glorious parp...

It echoed through time
Like an old nursery rhyme,

And it came from
a house on a farm.

Old MacDonald heard a parp...
E-I-E-I-O!
With a
Kwwrk
Blrrp
here...
Kwwrk!
Blrrp!
Pweep!
Wrrrb!
Get creative!
Do whatever you like,
and make some gold-
medal-winning parps!
1

and a
Pweep Wrrrb
there...
Who did it? We just don't know.

The cow

and the duck

and the man with the beard,

Looked through the window and smiled.

And there with his toys
Was the source of the noise...

A strangely familiar child!

THE END